Birth

Birth

Aaron van Donkelaar

2014

ISBN 978-0-9937171-1-6

Though great was King Enoch, his strength could not overcome a land so besought by discord and drought. For the sake of Edom, wise King Enoch abandoned his life and approached the throne of God. The kingdom was pardoned her sins, and the rains returned.

T HE golden light of dawn could first be seen as only a glow behind the eastern mountains. Silently it reached over the darkness below to touch the peaks rising in the west. It slowly descended onto a small cluster of buildings. Starting from a steeple, it flowed, stone on stone, down to the beads of the monastery's bells. The strike of a hammer brought an end to the stillness of night. The hammer struck again and again, causing the bells to call out, their voices announcing that God had wrought a new light to shine over all of Edom. The bells sang to its people in the valley below, in their homes and in their fields. The bells heralded the creation of light and honoured the angels who, even now, extinguished the sparks that had fallen from God's anvil onto the night sky, the stars that faded with the rising sun.

A shepherd at the base of the foothills watched a shooting star, a final spark, sweep across the heavens. He brought a fist to his chest, the sign of St. Enoch, and paused at the heralding of the light. He looked to the monastery with a thankful heart and turned to watch the rising sun. His flock, too, knew the sound of the bells and were glad. They paused their grazing, raised their heads, and looked expectantly to the glowing mountains.

A farmer to the east, already hard at work, also stopped to watch the sunrise. He raised his hands towards heaven and gave thanks. He looked at the dry fields that surrounded him, and prayed for the harvest to come. Turning, he reached for his hoe and sunk its head deep into the soil, labouring to fulfill his needs by the strength God had given him.

At the centre of the valley the ringing of the bells was followed by the sound of great doors being opened, movements of chain and lock allowing entrance into the granite-walled capital. Vendors stirred, scraping pole on stone, raising their stalls and laying out their goods.

The bells marked the end of the monastery's morning meditation; their voice was the first of each day. So it was that Elijah waited, as all those of his Order, withholding the clutter of words from his mind, listening intently for the voice of God.

He sat, as he did each morning, in the monastery gardens to await the sunrise. He had watched with anticipation as the light moved towards the bells, and joined in their song at the first toll, giving thanks with each echoed reprisal. He sought mercy with the fading stars and again fell silent as the final toll ceased, until the only light was that of the sun. Elijah dwelt in its warmth for a moment and, rising, walked towards the orchard to begin his work.

The trees were in full bloom, offering the promise of a fruitful fall harvest. Accompanied by the buzzing bees, the young novice inspected each one, examining their leaves and smelling their flowers. He continued into the garden. It had not yet begun to yield the spring crop, but it was green with new growth. Only kale and carrots, protected by straw and snow throughout the winter, were still harvested from the ground. Grape vines clung to the outer fence, rising above the weeds that had begun to surround their base. Elijah picked up a hoe from the dirt and drew them away. Kneeling, he began to reclaim those plants who had intertwined too closely with the unwanted growth. His back was warmed by the sun, and his hands were covered by the moist earth.

A breeze filled with the aroma of hay and lilac brushed past Elijah, causing him to pause in his work. Scents from the valley were often carried on the wind that drifted through the monastery grounds. They rustled in the trees, and then continued on their way, carrying their memory onward to whomever they met.

Hay and lilac. They returned Elijah to the days of his youth, working on his father's farm with his elder brother, Simeon. There, too, this pairing of scents had accompanied his labour. The lilac bushes grew tall between the barn and the fields, and every spring their perfume had filled the breeze that had relieved him while he lifted bales for the animals.

Lost in reflection on the monastery grounds, Elijah did not notice Father Zechariah approach. The priest paused at the edge of the vegetable garden, contemplating the young novice with pride. Elijah and his elder brother had come to him in need when Elijah had been only twelve. Zechariah had arranged for him to tend the garden and his brother to tend a flock in the valley below. In time, Elijah had joined the monastery as a novice, but his love of the earth had never faded.

Zechariah looked down at the leather-bound book in his hands. Their Order understood gardens, and their humble gardeners were highly blessed. Zechariah had also been a gardener as a novice, but unlike most others, the position had taken him far from the monastery. An unknown and ancient garden had been found within the wilds of the southern forest, and he had been sent to catalogue its remains. There he discovered that the Garden of St. Enoch, the prize of the old kingdom, had been returned to them. He opened the book to a map of the garden, its pages coloured with the ochres of that holy earth, and considered Elijah once more.

Unaware of his audience, Elijah remained kneeling in the soil, distracted by the flight of an orange-winged butterfly. He heard the mourning swallow sing its sullen song. He shut his eyes and felt the breath that entered his body.

Elijah thought often of his mother during such moments. She had been lost during a failed labour in his youth, forever tainting for him the hopeful with a shade of sorrow. The scent of lilacs, however, took his thoughts to a day years after, the day the barn had caught fire and his father was killed. His father had sent Simeon and the dogs to drive a steer to the butcher, and Elijah to the miller with a load of rye. Elijah had seen the smoke from a distance. He had whipped the horse until it bled, desperately beseeching it to go ever faster by the sting of his whip. They arrived too late, and the flames could not be stopped. The smell of hay and lilac still hung in the air, drifting among the smoke. It had been a long time before he could again savour their scent.

"Good morning Eli," interrupted Father Zechariah.

"Good morning, Father," said Elijah, rising to greet his patriarch.

"It is difficult to ignore so wonderful a world, is it not?" said Zechariah, misunderstanding the novice's distraction.

"My apologies, Father, I shouldn't neglect my duties."

"You misunderstand my purpose, Elijah. Come, walk with me a moment."

Placing the book in his satchel, Father Zechariah began to stroll through the garden. Elijah walked beside him, watching the old priest evaluate each plant that they passed. Occasionally Zechariah would pause, bend, and draw a flower to his bearded face, or pull an herb and taste thoughtfully of its leaf.

"You have done wonderful work on this garden," said Zechariah.

"God is the creator," said Elijah. "I take no credit."

"Nonsense," said Zechariah, "where your hands have laboured, the beauty of God's works are obvious to all.

"Life is as a garden, Eli. Much in the same way that we help form our surroundings, so do gardens form their own soil. For the growth of today will, in time, become the earth from which the next generation matures. Likewise, as we tend our gardens, so does God choose to tend to us. For we do not force the plants to bloom or flourish, but rather we only set their surroundings towards that end. The plants can always refuse our design, but it seems that at the gift of your hands, they would rather seek to fulfill it."

Father Zechariah paused as he came to the mountainside that rose up to define the garden's eastern edge, its granite carved to form the Tomb of St. Hannah. Its large, round entrance had been opened in preparation, but the daylight did not penetrate into its cavern. Its archway was embraced by the massive sculpture of a man, whose stone-chiselled tears shed eternally over the departed. His great grey eyes watched the priest and the novice with imploring mystery.

"Is it true," asked Elijah, "that prior to being ordained, you spent a month of prayer and fasting in the catacombs?"

"It is an old tradition," said Zechariah.

"What's it like in St. Hannah's Tomb?"

Zechariah met the statue's gaze as he replied: "From here, the entrance of the Tomb, all you can see is its darkness. The sounds of the world deaden as you step into its shadows and the sun's warmth is taken from you. The darkness deepens, and the air grows stale. But beyond these trials, you come to a place of great beauty. The air clears, and there is light, deep in the crypt. Water, too. You are surrounded by those who have come before us. Their bodies lie asleep, bone on cold stone, but through prayer their spirits, alive in the service of God, come to you. They sustain and guide you, testing the weight of your commitment and the fortitude of your compassion.

"The elders and I have been discussing your work," he said, turning to Elijah. "We have decided to assign you to a greater task. It will take you from us for a time, but it is a worthy endeavour."

"What am I to do?" asked Elijah. "Where am I to go?"

"In a week we will go to the forest at the far side of the valley," said Zechariah. "The explanation of our travel is long, and Barnabas departs us tonight. You and I will discuss our journey, but not today, for now my place is at his side."

The priest's departure left Elijah alone at the Tomb. He looked deeply into the sculpture's weeping eyes and wondered if they could see the path before him.

T HE palace was set behind fortified walls, its foundation laid on stone that delved deep into the earth. The king's council sat before him with stoic composure, their guarded minds hidden behind invisible walls that went deeper still. Tapestries deadened their silence among the stone, still cold in the morning sun.

The council, though many, was as one: a uniform-clad pack of generals who sought to abate their king. They feared and hated him; their malevolent thoughts fed on their suffering kingdom. But the sedition of their hearts remained tempered, for the King of Edom was wise and his foresight vast. He deflected their dissent with reason and measure, guiding their protest towards his own end. And so the king's council sat in unity, not only in fear and hate, but in reverence and respect. When they spoke, their opinion was as one. When they were silent, their unvoiced words whispered dissent in the ear of the king.

"The wars have ended," said one general.

"Drought ravages our land," said another.

"We need food, not soldiers," spoke a third.

"Our wars did not end because we made peace," said the king, his great white staff held firmly in his hand. "We have subdued, but not broken, our neighbours. If we appear weak, war will rise again. My armies require the payment promised them."

"Soldiers are costly," insisted the first general.

"We have been at war many years," said the other.

"We have no gold," concluded the third.

It was at this moment that Father Gideon entered. Duties of the court priests had increased since the king's inauguration at the order of the queen. Neither noble, nor strong, Gideon's appearance was as amber among iron. The warm ochres of his garb were at odds with the grey uniforms surrounding the stone table; their colours paled and devalued beside the crisp cut of military men. Gideon took his seat while the king watched, the monarch seeing the answer to his puzzle.

"Father Gideon," said the king calmly, "your golden robes remind us of the wealth that the priesthood is to us all. Welcome to my council."

"Your Majesty," said a general, slowly focusing on Gideon's clothing, "the temple is rich."

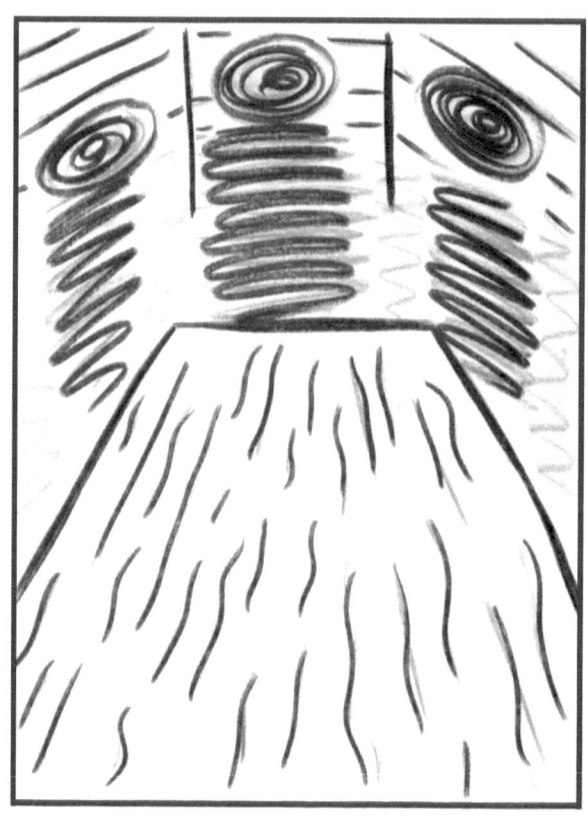

"We have defended it for many years," said another.

"Now let *it* pay for the protection of our soldiers," added a third.

"Impossible," said Gideon, taken aback. "We use our wealth for the work of God, the charity of His children. The king has already stopped our burnt offerings. Will you insult the Most High further, by waging war with His tithe?"

"I would not have food turned to ash while my people starve," said the king. "This has been decided. And are not all my people God's children?"

"They are," said Gideon.

After a brief silence, a general asked, "Do you not administer your tithe for the well-being of those children?"

"We do."

Another spoke up, a growing clarity in his voice, "If they are starving, will you grow them food?"

"As we are able."

"What if you are not able?" demanded a third.

"We buy what we cannot create."

"I see little difference," said the king, satisfied. "We will use the tithe to save God's children. Priests are not soldiers. You cannot protect my people. As food bought to stave death, the tithe will be used to keep my people from harm."

The generals' voice rose among the priest's protest.

"The people need more than soldiers," said Gideon. "Soldiers cannot feed them."

"By soldiers' strength, my people will not starve," said the king. "With strong arms, we will take what we cannot grow."

Z ECHARIAH entered the chapel through its southern door. It was the season of Jubilee, and the sanctuary was decorated in green and gold cloth, whose colours gave a supernatural warmth to the light of spring. An elderly priest dressed in ceremonial garments knelt in the alcove on the chapel's north face. Zechariah came and knelt beside him.

"Is it time?" asked the priest.

"Not yet, Barnabas," said Zechariah, "but soon."

The icon before them depicted the last days of St. Enoch. Its border showed gaunt figures working barren fields while armies fought beneath distant mountains. Its centre, however, showed the king poised in royal garments, standing in his court unaffected by the strife that surrounded him. He held a golden chalice raised towards the sky with his eyes fixed heavenward.

"When did you last consider this work?" asked Barnabas. "It was once so obvious to me. I could feel the weight of St. Enoch's cup, imagine its metal against my lips. The taste of its poison was on my tongue. I was a part of this icon. Our faithful act was so clear. I had paid it little heed these past years, however, and now that my lot is drawn I have returned to it for strength."

"Do you see it differently now?"

"There is a gulf that I can no longer cross. Now that I am to follow in the king's blessed footsteps, I cannot imagine even standing in his court. The need for his sacrifice has not changed, but I cannot find tranquility. Now that I need this comfort, it is lost."

"Soon you will find peace."

"In truth, Zechariah, I did not expect to be chosen. It is an honour, but you and I have been passed over for so many years, with many the younger who have gone on before us. I had begun to suspect that God had some other part for us to play."

"I will miss your company," said Zechariah, "but this is the moment that God has chosen. The timing of God is mysterious, but in His time all things will be made right."

"I do wish I could have lived to see fruit restored to the Garden of St. Enoch, the glory of that place . . . " Barnabas trailed off.

". . . is but a pale semblance of the glories that await you," interrupted Zechariah. "Today you will share in the first fruits of God. You will drink heavenly wine from your own golden cup and eat fruit from His eternal orchard. Your soul will feed upon the very light of God."

The other elders, also dressed in ceremonial robes, had begun to enter. Barnabas turned back to the icon and closed his eyes as, united in a reverent song of lament, the elders laid the ascension vessels upon the altar. One poured fine wine into a golden pitcher, another transferred extracts of hemlock and nightshade into a silver goblet. A third polished an ornate dagger. Central to the altar was placed a golden cup and a scroll, a seal and a silver bowl of melted beeswax.

Zechariah rose and went to them. Barnabas soon followed, each elder embracing him with a holy kiss before he solemnly knelt down. They prayed to God and placed oil on Barnabas' head. They surrounded him with a cloud of incense, and wept over him until the ringing of the bell.

The elders listened in silence to each toll, until the final note had been struck and its echo ceased, fading like dyed cloth left in the sun. When even the candles stopped their flickering dance, the chapel grew still to watch the giving of life.

Barnabas stood up and walked to the altar. He looked down at the gold and silver vessels before him. Into the divine silence he spoke:

"We give all that we have," he said, "in the hope of the people's reconciliation with God."

He lifted the golden cup from the altar and turned to the others. Peace befell him at last and, as many before, he said, "I will drink of death, that God may hear their cry."

The procession of elders left the chapel in stoic composure, each carrying one of the vessels. Barnabas carried the poison and Zechariah the golden cup. Citizens and officials, scattered amongst a priestly gathering, intently watched the elders approach the Tomb of St. Hannah.

Elijah watched from the edge of the crowd. He watched the line of elders approach and place each item on the slab in front of the Tomb, beneath the weeping stone giant. He watched Father Barnabas raise a scroll and heard him pray in a loud voice:

"As St. Enoch before me, I beseech mercy on behalf of the suffering people. Great God, ruler of heaven above and earth below, forgive us our sinful ways, send the rain once more."

The priest returned the scroll to the stone and reached for the small dagger. He drew its blade swiftly across the palm of his hand, catching his blood in the silver bowl and turning the golden tones of its beeswax a bright vermilion. Barnabas formed a seal on the scroll and placed it in the ornate canister that would bear his message, fastening it across his chest and over his shoulder.

He then poured the wine from the pitcher to the cup.

"We drink of the fruit You have given."

Barnabas added the poison to his cup and lifted it high.

"We partake of our own destruction, the works of our labour."

The rich sound of Barnabas' voice rose in song. The old priest sang praises to God: a hymn to celebrate a joyful departure. It was a strange

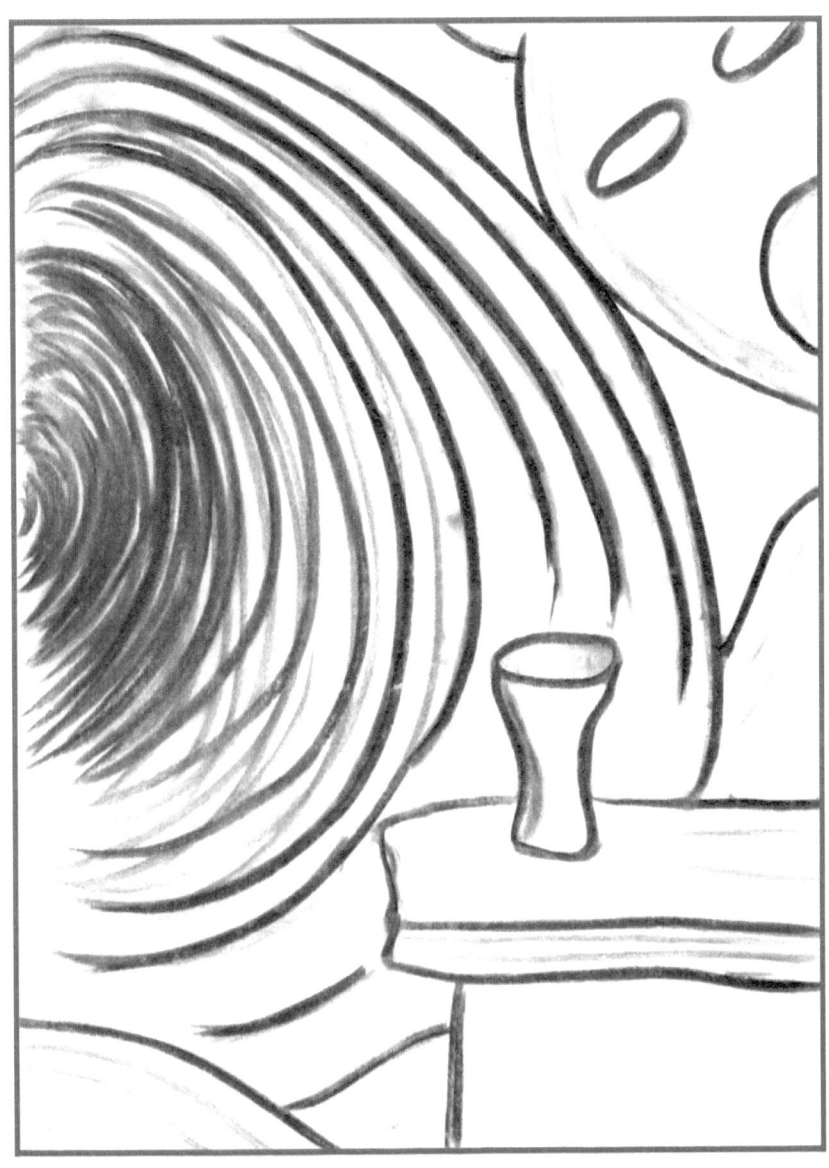

sight, thought Elijah, the old priest giving praise, overshadowed by the great weeping statue who lamented his journey.

Barnabas spoke in practiced verse:

> *Through dark of death, we pass away:*
> *this loss of life, our noblest deed.*
> *God's righteous will, we ask to sway:*
> *His ear we bend, in greatest need.*
>
> *The sufferings of this world seek voice:*
> *it pains our heart, our souls compel.*
> *Though we will die, we will rejoice.*
> *For by this gift, we sins dispel.*

At the closing of the hymn, Elijah watched as Barnabas raised the chalice to his lips and emptied the cup.

Aware of the poison that now flowed through his veins, Barnabas tested the scroll was secure about him. He made three paces towards the Tomb and turned to face the setting sun. With due wonder he then raised his right hand. Looking past those gathered, he turned and stepped out of sight, into the darkness.

THE monastic corridor was housed in the tallest of the palace towers, from whose windows prayers could be offered over the people of Edom. The remnants of a bridge, partially refurbished, linked it to the king's tower. Peering across the broken divide, the residents of each tower were reminded of the queen whose influence had abetted its renewal. Her passing, however, had left the repairs unfinished, and had only served to increase the gulf between them.

Within the corridor stood a shamed Father Gideon, his eyes downcast before his livid brother. Father Obadiah's rasped voice could be heard decrying both his brethren and his king. His gaunt figure had weathered the wrath of kings for generations, and his condemnations were among the few that the present monarch would tolerate.

"He cannot take God's tithe," said Obadiah. "Will his insults never cease? He has already stolen our burnt offering. Does he deliberately seek to offend God?"

"The people are starving," said Gideon, meekly. "There is not enough food to burn. The king seeks only to protect his people."

"Righteous offerings are not wrought from excess!" rebuked Obadiah. "They are given in thanksgiving and faithful anticipation of God's sustenance. The king, in his arrogance, jeopardizes our divine covenant."

"Holy rights can be neglected for a time in the service of the people," said Gideon. "We take time from prayer to work the fields. As we feed the starving, he is protecting the weak."

"Working the fields is as holy prayer," snapped Obadiah, "a communion with God in which our supplication embodies our toil. The king's actions are no prayer. He seeks to protect the people? God is our defence. He sacrifices the favour of the Great Protector to gain the strength of men."

"Our king would disagree. His usage is reasonable."

"It may be reasonable, but it is not right."

"What would you have him do? We are surrounded by enemies."

"Better to be surrounded by enemies than to make a foe of your own people," said Obadiah. "Even if God does not act against us, the people of Edom rightly grow restless in their hunger. The strength of the king's army should be put to digging wells, its expense spent on the acquisition of food."

"Have you discussed this with him?" asked Gideon.

"I have spoken, but he will not listen. He cannot hear the truth of what I say. In the end, the king simply refuses to act in faith on that which is beyond his understanding."

Silence fell between the two priests. A bell rang in the courtyard below them, announcing the third quarter of the day.

"It is time for evening prayer," said Obadiah. "You are dismissed. Pray that God's wisdom would reign in our day."

The murmurs of Obadiah's prayer followed Gideon as he walked to his cell. There he, too, knelt before his God. He asked for mercy. He pleaded for rain. Above all, he begged for the return of peace to Edom.

HALF a mile above the valley floor, Simeon left the main path that led up onto the monastery. He pushed through familiar brush and emerged onto a small outcrop that extended from the rock face. Taking rest on a well-formed stone, he sat in the shade of a juniper tree and looked out upon the kingdom. Mountains defined Edom, and nowhere could they not be seen: white-haired giants, standing guard over the kingdom. And in the centre of the valley floor, with its walls as a crown atop the mesa that was the mountain's little brother, rose the city of Edom.

Simeon's gaze, however, lingered neither on the mesa nor on the city, but turned towards the pasture land. Using the city and a small patch of oak trees, he carefully counted four lengths. There, just beyond his vision, would be a small earthen hut, and Tabitha, his wife, would be inside. She would be spinning the wool taken from the spring shear.

Simeon closed his eyes and imagined the pulse of the wheel. He could hear Tabitha's voice, quietly singing to its rhythm as she worked. She would, from time to time, pause in her labour, and he would listen to the sound of the cloth that moved against her skin as she gently rubbed her belly. A timbre of joy would rise in her song, as she felt for the child that grew inside her.

As he, too, paused, Simeon could feel his own joy spring up at the thought of their child. Simeon reached into his satchel and withdrew the last of the winter apples. He was looking forward to telling Elijah; his younger brother's happiness would equal their own. With a thankful heart, Simeon cut a slice of the fruit and ate it with appreciation. The drought had made fruit a valuable commodity, one within the reach of only Edom's elect. Yet Elijah had provided for them, sharing from the monastery's bounty, unknowingly providing for the growth of their unborn child.

Simeon had been twelve when he first climbed this path. Recently orphaned, he and his brother had nowhere else to turn. They had made each step alone and in fear, but their isolation quickly vanished once they reached the monastery. Father Zechariah, in particular, had become as family to them, caring for them and teaching them as his own. Simeon had made the trip to the monastery many times since that first day. It was like going home.

Cleaning his knife on his pant leg, Simeon rose from his seat and returned to the path. The climb was steep, but Simeon found it enjoyable, drawing strength from the anticipation of a long-awaited visit with his brother and the other monks.

The monastery grounds were on the largest plateau of the western mountains. Filled with a bounty of fertile acres, it was ideally suited to sustain the Order of St. Enoch. Its structures were few: a chapel, a dormitory, some storehouses and some barns. All had wooden roofs and, with the exception of the chapel, had been built using fieldstone. Cut stone from the Tomb of St. Hannah had been used for the chapel. Waist-high walls defined orchards and gardens, separated roosters and their flocks, and kept the goats from wayward entrance into the holy cloisters. The mountains rose and fell sharply from the edge of the grounds, with only the mountain path that Simeon travelled allowing access to the community.

A group of priests smiled welcomingly as he entered, but Simeon did not see Elijah among them. He exchanged greetings with those present, giving them a gift of mutton and receiving their blessings in return. He carried on instinctively to the garden, calling out as he entered, "Little brother?"

Nearby, Elijah smiled at the sound of his brother's voice. He was not far from Simeon, harvesting rhubarb on his knees, sheltered by the branches of an elderberry bush. With boyish amusement, Elijah silently lingered in his hiding place as Simeon instinctively drew nearer.

"Little brother?" said Simeon again, feeling his brother's presence.

Elijah hopped to his feet and with theatrical enthusiasm wiped the dirt from his hands onto his robe.

"Ah! Little brother, there you are," said Simeon. "It's good to see you."

"And you," said Elijah, embracing him heartily, ensuring the dirt had well-committed to his brother's clothing.

Simeon laughed, and skillfully tripped his brother onto the ground. "Not even the king has a garden so green," he observed, taking stock of the garden as Elijah sat in the dirt.

"We are fed by mountain waters, the rains do not affect us here." said Elijah, reaching for Simeon's offered hand, and adding hastily, "What we do, we do in God's service, and He blesses us richly."

"If only my deeds were so clearly aligned with the will of God," said Simeon, visibly amused.

"In the words of St. Joab: 'All human labours contrive to complete the will of God'," countered Elijah. "It's inevitable."

"If true, that's both a comfort and a distress," said Simeon. "But such musing can wait, Eli, I bring wonderful news. Tabitha is with child."

"Praise God! When do you expect the birth?"

"If all goes well, in several months. The winter, however, hasn't been easy on our child. I came not only to share in my happiness, but to ask for your prayers. Tabitha has fears of complications; the child is moving less and less with each passing day."

"And of course you'll have them." said Elijah, "But I am to depart the monastery tomorrow! I won't be able to visit for some time, but you and Tabitha will never be far from my thoughts and always in my prayers. We'll have to celebrate when I return."

"Certainly," said Simeon, "but where are you going? You've never travelled before."

"To the old woods," said Elijah. "Beyond that, I don't know. But come, there are some kale and other preserves to spare. Tabitha needs more than just mutton to eat."

The brothers walked back to the storehouses. Elijah went inside and returned with a large sack of food. He held it out to Simeon, who paused as his hands touched its cloth.

"I have said it many times," he said, "but, thank you, little brother."

"I only give of the gifts I have been given," said Elijah. "All praise be to God. We are both blessed. Take this food and give Tabitha my greetings. I must prepare for my journey, but I'll send word when I return."

"Then I should depart and leave you to your provisions. Take care, Eli! May your journey be fruitful."

"Goodbye, Simeon," said Elijah.

Simeon waved farewell from the garden gate. He began to sing from the joy-filled song his wife had given him, amplified in thanksgiving to his brother and the Father above. As the mountain path took him from sight, the ever-circuitous wind carried his tune around rock and ridge, presenting it as a gift to Elijah. In response the novice knelt and closed his eyes, praising God for the divine metre of his song.

WHILST climbing each shadowed step, Obadiah muttered against any king who would interrupt his evening prayer. He lumbered past the royal guard and into the king's chamber, stopping a few steps into the room. Looking beyond a cluttered desk, Obadiah saw the king watching over his kingdom from his study terrace in the light of the setting sun. An empty chair faced the meal that, long turned cold, remained untouched on the table beside him. The wind blew forcibly, and while the king paid it no heed, his cup was made to fall. Its wine was lost against the stone.

"If God's light is born from the east," asked the king, "what is this western darkness that can extinguish its grace so readily?" He set a small copper box on the table and firmly righted his goblet. "Thank you for joining me, Father."

"It is my place to be at your call, Majesty," said Obadiah, glancing not without curiosity at the box.

"It is a compass," explained the king as he opened it, "one that is rare even among those few that exist. It has travelled the history of Edom, guiding our first kings onto this place and the founding of our kingdom. The sides of its case are etched with the map of a distant sea, forests and plains, the places from which we came long ago. At its centre is Edom, its mountains surrounding the mesa, and the lands of the northern kings.

"It was the queen's prized possession, for its history, yes, but also for the lesson she saw in it. It provided both a bearing and a course. With these, she said, any destination could be achieved. She had often carried this compass with her, even slept with it in her hands. She dropped it as she lay dying. It has not worked since."

Although at odds throughout his reign, the king held the old priest in high regard. Obadiah's thoughts were often in discord with the monarch's own, reasoned mind, but he would not have denied that the priest's insights had wisdom. His presence had in the past provided a commensurate soul, a counterbalance to the king's reason. But since the death of the queen, the priest's wisdom had become clouded from him. Queen Hannah had often been the break in these clouds, her presence letting the light pass between them. Without her, however, the king and the priest were increasingly unable to find common ground, leaving each to wish for the occasional whisper of Hannah's voice that the fog may be lifted.

The king took a seat and motioned that Obadiah should do the same.

"Tell me, priest, do you dream at night?" asked the king.

"Most nights, Your Majesty," said Obadiah.

"And what do you believe is the meaning of a dream?"

"There is no simple answer," replied the priest. "It would depend upon the dream. I suppose that some are warnings, others are reflections. In a dream, my spirit truly hears the voice of God."

"But where does my spirit go in the silence of a dreamless sleep?" asked the king.

"Only God could say, Your Majesty."

"If God speaks through our dreams," said the king, who had not dreamt in years, "He has long sent me an empty word."

"There are other echoes of His voice. Have you sought Him in other ways?"

"You are the priest," said the king, rising from his seat. "Communion with God is your business. You have my leave. Thank you for your counsel, priest."

"As you wish, Your Highness," said Obadiah uncertainly, but eager to return to his prayers.

The king, with the departure of the priest, turned his gaze back to the horizon. The wind redoubled its earlier assault upon his cup, causing it to fall once more. This time he abandoned it to the stone, driven back to the confines of his study by the howling wind amidst the growing darkness.

ZECHARIAH had led Elijah and their mule halfway down the mountain path when they heard the monastery bells herald the new day. They turned to witness the first light flooding out of the monastery, flowing past them onto the valley floor. The pair descended in silence as the whole of Edom was washed in the golden morning sun.

Their arrival at the mountain base was met only by the brown, parched grass that had become so common to the drought-ridden land. They followed the dirt path onward, its grand, meandering course making

near-serpentine motions over the miles that passed beneath them. The mule's steady footsteps lofted dust in their wake. It hung in the air, lingering above the ground. Sustained by the wind, the dust lifted further from the road and attempted to move heavenward. But dust remained dust, and its weight resisted the wind. Unable to rise by its own strength, it fell onto the pastures behind them and coated the plants in their wake.

Withered grass became wizened crop as grassland turned to field at their approach to the city. Ancient bridges, several horses wide, flowed down from the mesa. The hard, parched road beneath the traveller's feet felt unbroken as they transitioned onto the unyielding ascent of stone. Looking up, Elijah could not help but wonder at the granite city from whose gates all the kingdom's paths seemingly streamed forward throughout the land.

Zechariah and Elijah entered the city from the north. Narrow streets twisted and turned as they made their way through the city. Elijah and Zechariah were soon at the central square, surrounded by merchants and beseeched by beggars. One man called out to them: "Father! Give me food! " and another: "Help me! I am starving!" Elijah began to reach into their mule's pack, but Zechariah stayed his hand.

"Our monastery cannot feed the whole world," he said.

Further into the crowd was another man. Prostrate on the stone, a chipped clay bowl was cupped in his shaking hands. It was Zechariah who retrieved food and, steadying his grip, placed it in his bowl.

"Father?" asked Elijah, a little further on.

"Yes," said Zechariah.

"Why didn't you give food to the others?" said Elijah.

"We must do what we can with what we are given." reminded Zechariah, "I felt that our supplies had another calling until I met that man. No one can feed the whole world, but we must not just feed ourselves."

"But, how did you know?" said Elijah, "How can you be so certain that to feed him was according to God's will, while you left the others to starve?"

"Certain?" said Zechariah. "Certainty was lost to me long ago. I have read about the ancient prophets who talked directly with God, and I have wept in yearning for such clarity of His voice: a path without doubt, a course not burdened by faith. But it is far too easy to think that then our actions would be clear – recall that the ancients, when given such commands, rarely obeyed. I am no greater than they. I do not have a ready answer as to why I chose one man over the others. I have not heard the voice of God. But faith remains. I can say only that it is this last man who moved my heart to pity. It is he to whom my spirit cried out."

A great fountain, now dry, paid tribute to King Enoch from the centre of the square. The mighty portrait of the king was carved with a sheaf of wheat held firmly to his side. His gaze was fixed on the eastern horizon, and his expression paid no heed to the knife with which he had pierced his own chest. Before the drought, clear water had flowed down his robes from the wound. Now merchants, who collected dew from the fields, sold their muddy waters by his feet.

"Even St. Enoch's robes have dried," said Zechariah, more to himself than Elijah.

"St. Enoch designed this city, centuries before its construction began," continued the priest, now turning to the novice, "yet he never saw one stone of its foundation laid."

"I didn't know," said Elijah, surprised.

"Yes," said Zechariah, "while the architects of other kings provided its details, and their craftsmen built its structures, it was St. Enoch who had seen the potential of this mesa and yearned for a great city here. In the time before Enoch, however, our history was filled with war, and our people had built a strong defence among the rocks and trees of the southern forest.

"Our times shape us, and define our priorities. The wars ended after Enoch. It was this peace that allowed the others to fulfill St. Enoch's

vision; resources once consumed by war were put to construction. Gold no longer bought military force, but paid for the prosperity of our people, a longer vision for their protection. The old city was abandoned, and a new age was born."

"Is the old city still there?" asked Elijah.

"A few pillars, an old mill and the ruins of a garden," said Zechariah, satisfied. "Tonight we sleep here in the city, but we will stand in that place before the sun sets tomorrow."

T HE king sat before his council, his staff held firmly in his hand.

"The people are rationed," said a general. "All go hungry."

"Our prisons overflow, and your people murmur against you," said another.

"We must act carefully, or rebellion will come to Edom," voiced a third.

"How many of my people are in prison?" asked the king.

"One in five," said a general.

"They are in walled camps on the plains," said the second.

"The camps are beyond capacity," said a third.

The king considered their response and said, "The camps are no longer to be fed."

"But, Your Highness, they are your citizens," said the first general.

"Do we have no other choice?" asked the second.

"We cannot starve our own people," said the third.

"I am the King," said the king sharply, "and they are my people. If you cannot bear my law, perhaps we will feed them your meals."

"It is reasonable," the first general agreed at length.

"We have no other choice," said the second.

The third general remained silent, but with a reluctant nod solemnly supported the wisdom of his monarch.

E LIJAH looked out across the city from the window of the monastic cell. The night-long light of hearths and lamps that filled the city denied the full onset of darkness, diminishing the presence of the stars. The rustling of the city, too, seemed to distance the novice from night's familiar silence. Wondering at this, he fixed his eyes on the heavens and counted the number of stars before the soon-brightening sky would drive them from his gaze.

"The city's light makes us blind," he whispered, pondering its meaning. "Yet the heavens still shine, just beyond our vision. God's light is ever present, but it can be seen most clearly in the darkness."

"It's the same with silence," he considered. "Silence lets us hear God. And fasting. Through hunger we taste the fruit of God."

In response, Elijah again quieted his thoughts. He listened to the stars' silence beyond the city's noise, holding their stillness in his mind. The sky grew brighter, but their silent vigil remained.

Zechariah tapped gently on his door and entered.

"Forgive my voice," he said softly, "but the city will open her gates with the sun. We should depart."

They left the monastic tower in silence, seen only by the ghostly presence of an elderly priest who nodded farewell at their parting. They reached the southern gate in twilight, and watched it open with the sun. The southern forest, visible from the height of the city, was lost to the

horizon as Zechariah and Elijah returned to the valley floor. The passing fields marked the distance, until trees again adorned the feet of the mountain before them. By late afternoon the travellers stood at the edge of the deep woods.

Fragments of cobblestone littered a subtle path into the forest, the remnants of an ancient road. Zechariah and Elijah made their way under the unbroken shadow of imposing trees. Zechariah moved with comfort, but Elijah could not look to the trees for the tangle of roots. Creaking pines called with scornful distemper through the dim light.

The tree's complaints fell back and held their distance as Zechariah and Elijah stepped into the light that flooded a small hollow. The trail of cobblestone branched into three paths, each heading towards a separate mountain summit.

"Do you know which way we are going?" asked Elijah.

"I do," said Zechariah and then spoke in rhyme:

> *The broken road leads home, my son,*
> *where Enoch's bones abide.*

> *Three brothers stand fore'er on guard:*
> *the royal kin will guide . . . .*

"The purple hue of Mount Cignus has long been associated with royalty," he said. "We follow it towards the old city."

They took the middle path towards Cignus and continued through the woods into the foothills. A scattering of granite boulders marked the end of the thick forest.

"The toes of Cignus," announced Zechariah:

> *. . . . His largest toe a secret hides,*
> *the glory of our past . . . .*

Carved into the stone beneath the shallow dirt, and hidden from the trail, Zechariah led them to a jet-veined tunnel that descended into the earth.

. . . . By black-veined skin in darkness deep,
true light we find at last.

Zechariah removed a torch from their mule's pack. Lighting it, he led the beast below. The tunnel was dark, even by firelight, and the reverberant clop of mule's hooves dampened with the shaft's twists and turns as they delved deeper into the earth.

Eventually, the rough tunnel grew level and its surfaces smooth. It widened slightly and, at the end of a short corridor, an arched doorway emerged. The doorway was exquisitely carved from the stone itself, its black surface offering no release from the darkness that surrounded them. Zechariah, however, extinguished his torch. To Elijah's growing wonder, glass adornment illuminated the door in purple flowers, lit from behind with a quiet and unwavering light.

"Old Edom was once a place of pilgrimage for our Order," said Zechariah. "That rhyme had guided us for centuries, until the kings deemed it disrespectful to the new city. They built a monument to Enoch and ordered this journey to cease. This path was lost in the passage of time. But, also with time, it was found."

Zechariah opened the door, revealing a large chamber—a crypt. An open archway opposite them revealed sunlit stairs, whose reflected light gave revered illumination to the entire tomb. Elijah studied the carved walls, whose imagery transitioned from scenes of famine and strife to tables of feast and serenity. He followed the water that flowed through the room and formed a pool at its centre. A great sarcophagus rose above the waters, and with awe he beheld the resting place of his king.

Zechariah and Elijah bowed before the ancient king and saint, giving praise and thanks to God. Neither spoke, but when Zechariah stood up and reverently walked to the archway and up the stairs, Elijah followed.

Stepping into daylight, Elijah stood in a sanctuary of broken walls.

"In my youth, " said Zechariah, "I was charged to seek the old city and her structures. I was given the rhyme, which led me to St. Enoch. Few are living who have seen this place."

Vine-covered statues and fountains sat ensconced by untended trees and bushes. Strange flowers bloomed with wild splendour among unknown birds whose imported parents were brought long ago at the pleasure of a king.

The Tomb of St. Enoch formed the foundation of a stone stage at the garden's head. Its entrance led prominently down into the earth, the adornment of its archway conveying steadfast homage to the king through the passing years.

"Do you know where you are?" asked Zechariah.

"I'm dumb with wonder," said Elijah.

"Welcome to the Garden of St. Enoch," said Zechariah. "The pronouncement of the king's sacrifice, from this stage, saw the birth of our Order. This is our source, for it is here that Enoch rests. It is here that our roots reside, for the world that surrounds us is an unkempt garden. And it is here in which we hope, for the flowers of our world, like these, need only a reason to bloom."

Elijah breathed deeply. He touched, in turn, stone and dirt, leaf and flower. He walked up the stage and looked out across the garden. Speechless, he turned to Zechariah.

"It is written," said the old priest, "that some of these plants were from the angels who nourished our land after the last great drought. They were seen to flower only once, at St. Enoch's death, but the most stoic of men were brought to tears by their beauty. Like the garden as a whole, they are less magnificent these days, but they do survive here still."

"Will you show me?" asked Elijah.

"You will find them in time," said Zechariah. "It is not right that this garden is in such disrepair, when it should represent the glory due our saint. The elders have ordained this garden to be restored. It is to be your charge, Elijah. Will you accept?"

"Gladly," said Elijah. "Such labour would be a joy."

"Good," said Zechariah, reaching into the mule's pack. He withdrew his old leather-bound book and passed it to Elijah. "This will help. These are the writings of my youth, my inquiry of the garden past. It is not complete, and there is much we do not know, but it should serve to guide you well."

"Thank you, Father," said Elijah, kissing his hand. "I'll restore it with all my strength."

"For the glory of God, I believe St. Enoch's splendour will shine here once more," said Zechariah. "For tonight, however, we must make camp. I will depart in the morning, and you will stay. Work hard. Return as necessary, but we will send further supplies. Request whatsoever you need. You have our full blessing and support."

"WE must speak, Your Highness," said Father Obadiah, blocking passage of the king's entourage.

"Of course," said the king, motioning his generals away.

"Is it true that you have ordered the prisoners unfed?" asked Obadiah.

"My dear priest," said the king, "your God has withheld the rain. We are quickly running out of food, and so someone must starve. We must follow the reasonable course."

"Such blind devotion is only fitting to deities," said Obadiah, "and reason makes for a poor God."

The king paused and said, "In the one hand I hold my people who have served me in obedience through this present hardship. In the other, I hold the criminals who have broken our laws, many of which were handed down by your God. Whom would you choose to die?"

"Many stole only so they would not starve."

"Is it still not stealing?"

"Is it still not killing?"

"Good, we are in agreement," said the king. "As there is a time to steal, so may there be a time to kill."

"There is still some food, Your Highness," pleaded Obadiah, "perhaps we do not need to take such drastic action."

"We are given foresight for a purpose, priest; it would be foolish to disregard its wisdom."

"It is *wrong*," insisted the priest with growing impatience.

"It is also wrong to idly sit and watch my people starve," said the monarch. "If a shepherd must slaughter sheep to feed his family, will he not select those who bore him the most wretched wool? Or will a farmer not choose the obstinate ox, who refused to plough? The matter is decided."

"Queen Hannah would have understood," said the priest in rash response.

"The queen is dead," said the king, flatly.

And he walked away, leaving Obadiah tight-fisted in impotent rage.

THE physicians of Edom were few, the advice of whom was often reserved only for the illnesses of the wealthy. The countryside, filled with poverty and superstition, held for them little appeal. Compensation was not only small among the common folk, but outside of the city the healers' wisdom was often given little heed. Royal edict, however, demanded that once each month the doctors of Edom, laden with remedies and knowledge, travel the whole of the valley to dispense their learning in charity.

Despite such inconvenience and expense, Isaac the physician revelled in his monthly journey, and took to the country like a child released from his daily chores. Reprieved of his nagging wife, liberated from his despondent children, Isaac travelled the roads with a leisurely gait, whistling his own private hymn of celebration.

Isaac had his usual route and his usual clients. He particularly enjoyed when the dairymaids fell ill—their cheese was delicious—or when the vintner had hives, and he could receive a properly balanced Pinot in peace. For these, their minor ailments brought him his greatest pleasures, but he ignored no one, and a red cloth hung outside the shepherd's cabin bid him to come.

"The king's gift to his subjects, I come. What ailments afflict his people?" he announced in accordance with the king's dictates and, with a smile all his own, added, "What gifts can we share to resurrect some pleasure to this life?"

Simeon and Tabitha welcomed him warmly. Simeon stepped outside, and Tabitha began to speak of her concerns to their guest.

"Our child hasn't moved in many weeks. I've begun to worry," she said.

"Please lie down," instructed the physician.

Isaac took a lotion from his bag and applied it to her belly.

"Let us see if he has a temper," he said. "It will be cold. The child will kick in displeasure."

The chilling of her womb wrenched at Tabitha's heart. The burning emotion of her tears, their heat unmatched against the departing warmth of her belly, fell idly down her cheek. Her womb, a tomb within her, descended ever deeper into the cold, yet no kicks protested against her walls, no twisting child railed in discontent.

"Let us be more direct," said the physician. "I will listen for a heartbeat."

Isaac removed a horn-shaped instrument from his bag. He placed its bell against Tabitha, where the bulge of the child lay motionless.

Tabitha strained to hear, desperately seeking a pulse beyond her own, but silence alone met her waiting ear as the physician repositioned his horn again and again.

"I am sorry," said Isaac, shaking his head. "These are difficult times."

"What do you mean?"

"Your child no longer lives," he said plainly. "We must take steps to protect you. The child must be removed."

"You will not touch my child," said Tabitha, sitting up and protectively moving her arms in front of her belly.

"We should speak with your husband," said the physician.

Isaac opened the door, and Simeon entered.

"There are complications," Isaac said to him. "At this stage in your wife's pregnancy, any healthy child should be visibly active, and even the weakest should have a heartbeat. This drought has been hard on us all, and the pregnant require much more than this land has to offer. I am sorry. Tabitha's body was unable to support a child, and he has been lost."

"That can't be," said Simeon, watching the silent tears fall from Tabitha's eyes.

"A failed pregnancy is always difficult," said the physician, "but when it does occur, the child should pass naturally from the mother's body. If this does not happen, as for Tabitha, she herself is in danger. For her protection, we must force labour."

"It is too soon, our child wouldn't live."

"The child is already dead."

"You can't be sure of that."

"I understand you are upset," said Isaac, "but I can assure you, you must terminate this pregnancy or you risk your wife. I am a physician. My knowledge can save her."

"What if your knowledge is wrong?" asked Simeon. "Is the death of our child forgivable because you thought it inevitable? No! You believe our child is dead, but if we force miscarriage, that fate becomes fact. We won't unnecessarily cause your knowledge to become truth."

"The sooner we act, the less damage will be done to your wife," said the physician, taking a glass jar from his bag and placing it in Simeon's hands. "A strong tea of these leaves, taken twice daily, will force Tabitha's labour within three days. This must be done."

"You must make her understand," insisted Isaac, not unkindly motioning to Tabitha. "I am trying to help you."

"But you must understand," said Simeon, watching Tabitha shake her head, "your help risks all that is precious to us."

"I am sorry," said the physician. "It is not a perfect world. We must sometimes step out in faith, trusting those given knowledge beyond our own. Believe me, your child is dead. We must now save your wife. We must act to save those who are still in our care."

"I cannot follow your counsel any more than my wife would," replied Simeon. "Its price is too high. We will not harm our child."

"I will say it once more," said the physician. "Your child has already left you. Do you wish to lose your wife also? Or do you, Tabitha, wish to make a widower of your husband? Please consider my words: take the treatment. I will call again next month."

THORNS had overgrown St. Enoch's garden. They caused Elijah's hands to bleed as he worked the garden, but only strengthened his resolve as the weeds gave way to the black earth and long-overshadowed plants were prominent once more. Birds sang joyfully overhead, praising Elijah's work and that of their creator.

A whisper on the wind called Elijah's name. He rose and walked up the stone platform, following its voice. The sun cast long shadows from behind him. Looking out he saw a vision of King Enoch walking through the garden with a small copper box cupped in his hands. His eyes were fixed upon it, his head tilted down. Merchants, soldiers, priests and generals stood along the path, each speaking as he passed them by, but the king paid them no heed. The shadows loomed over him, blotting out the purple hues of his robes and paling the colour of his skin. The gathered crowd called louder as he moved further into the darkness, but the king's focus did not leave his hands.

Elijah watched the king stumble.

"No," the novice said in breathless horror.

And the king, hearing his voice, looked up and saw the sun. Darkness covered his body, but a golden ray now lit his face. The monarch approached where Elijah stood, his eyes set on the light as he was carried by shadows into the Tomb beneath him.

As the vision faded, Elijah's thoughts remained with his king. He stepped down from the platform and gazed into the blackness of St. Enoch's Tomb. The light from the garden penetrated within, he recalled, but, remaining in the light, all he could see was darkness.

Century-old vines gripped the pillars that raised the platform above the Tomb's entrance. Marble figures, though worn with time, still issued the presence of power from between each post. They had been carved in the identical likeness of a royal guard, each erected to stand watch over their king. Their vigil had revealed them, however, and time had uniquely weathered each stone. One face appeared proud, and another noble.

The figure at the head of the row drew Elijah's attention. Its degraded remains, entwined in ivy, were eroded much further than any of the others. One of its arms, fallen from the body, lay on the ground, its hand grasping out from the foliage. Its storm-swept face bore no expression at all. Elijah paused and considered its remains.

"Was your stone so different?" he wondered. "If the course of the wind had changed, could you have been another?"

Elijah cut the ivy from the statue and cleared the leaves from the ground. The glint of metal caught his eye from beneath the cleared foliage. Digging, Elijah pulled a pewter cup from the statue's base. Washing it in a puddle, he held the cup to the light and examined the intricate patterns that faintly shone from beneath a millennium of scratches. No such subtleties remained on the statue, he considered, yet its broken limbs and worn features still betrayed the care with which it had been crafted. In silence, it spoke the chorus of years, proving the merit of its vigil by its weary, but unwavering, endurance. Elijah stood by it and looked out across the garden whose untended growth exposed the ardent spirit that lay within its ancient cultivated kin. Their magnificent, broad leaves cast a shadow of doubt on Elijah's mind.

"Who directs the unkempt plant?" he wondered. "Does the gardener simply impede the hand of God?"

As if in answer, Elijah saw the corner of Zechariah's leather-bound book protruding from his satchel. He opened it to see sketches of the garden's glorious past. He again considered the garden before him. It bore the triumph of the plants who had flourished, but also the loss of those who had withered beneath them, those who, unaided, had become dust at the expense of the untended others. Satisfied, he returned to his work, releasing paths held captive and walls long buried. He uprooted and pruned, transplanted and restored.

He looked at the fruit of his labour and said, "Surely the gardener can also be the hand of God."

OBADIAH burst into Gideon's cell.

"The king will be accountable," he said with anger, "whether by man or by God. Lives cannot be cast aside without consequence!"

Gideon quietly rose from his desk and closed the door. He turned to his brother.

"So you have heard the king's plan to extend the people's food?" he said calmly.

"The people? It is the people he intends to starve."

"Some will starve, yes, but many will benefit from their sacrifice. The king did not make his decision lightly. We may regret it, but it is reasonable. Ours is to comfort those who will suffer."

"Are we to justify these faithless acts?" asked Obadiah, "The king's orders make sense, but they are not good. Reason must ever be bound with principle, and no course of logic can rightly overcome our moral duties. What reason is there to faith? What sense to compassion?"

"Even the compassionate require food," pleaded Gideon.

"We have fed our bodies," said Obadiah, "and thereby starved our souls."

ELIJAH felt his faith blossom like the flowers around him as he claimed back the most holy space of his Order. Over several months he had developed his own set of rituals, beginning each day by the waters in St. Enoch's Tomb, and closing each night under the heavens above. Elijah reclaimed the wild garden between these sacramental moments, resurrecting its walkways from the earth and restoring its prodigal sons after their wayward centuries of growth. Each plant was returned to its place, and those not written into the garden from its beginning were pulled, save for some hemlock which Elijah transferred from the monastery to a place near the Tomb's entrance.

"It is truly a wonder," Zechariah had said during his last visit, as he resupplied Elijah's camp. "In the stillness of this beautiful solitude, the voice of God suffers no contest. He can be heard on the wind and seen in the flowers.

"Yet we do not achieve salvation alone," he had continued, "and though a single bird's song is most fair, it is the flock that flies the farthest. Our spirits need both community and seclusion. Return to the monastery,

Eli. You have been alone too long. When next you need supplies, come to us. Be among your brethren and be strengthened by your community for a few days. Then you will return to your labour renewed."

And so, emerging from the forest two weeks later, Elijah was faced with the brown realities of drought. A palette of lifeless hues painted the valley, their only reprieve the bone-white stone of the bustling city.

But life continued in the valley, and with great pleasure Elijah saw his brother, Simeon, still a great distance away. Simeon's arms were held high as he directed his dogs. His animals moved with the swaying of his hands, played like a living instrument, to whose tune they could not help but dance. Elijah watched their music unfold as his flock was herded for the evening.

Elijah drew nearer and noted with concern a change in Simeon's familiar motions. His arms, usually so swift, appeared heavy. His voice, so strong, sounded tired. The dogs before him seemed as but an afterthought as Elijah interpreted his brothers song. Joy returned, however, as Simeon noticed Elijah and jubilantly heralded his approach.

"Little brother!" he said. "It's been too long. I haven't seen you since you travelled south. How is the garden?"

"I have seen God through its redemption," said Elijah, leaving his concerns behind. "My labours have been blessed, and the garden is being restored like a temple around me. I wish I could share it with you, but that will have to wait. How is Tabitha?"

"Tabitha is fine, for now," said Simeon quietly, a weight returning to his shoulders. "There are concerns. The child hasn't moved for some time. She may also be at risk."

"I'm sorry," said Elijah. "I shouldn't have been gone so long."

"There is little to be done, little brother. We wait and we pray."

"But it is not a burden you should bear alone."

"It's good that you know," said Simeon. "Pray God's mind may be flexible. The child's state is hidden, and Tabitha is alive. There is hope."

"God will hear our request," said Elijah.

"I know," said Simeon. "He always does. Thank you, little brother. Truly, I didn't expect you today. It is a gift. But the sun is setting, and I must return to Tabitha. Will I see you tomorrow?"

"I'll be at the monastery a few days," said Elijah, "but I'll join you soon."

Elijah watched his brother's flock slowly migrate into the horizon. A familiar wind blew in from the city. It met Elijah where he stood, his gaze cast across the land in imagination, watching his brother journey home to the arms of his wife. The wind offered Elijah its scents of stories, but it was unable to move him from the thought of Simeon.

His brother's words spoke of hope, but his voice bore none. A trembling in Simeon's voice echoed in Elijah's ear and lingered in his thoughts. God must be made aware of Simeon's plight, yet Elijah knew of only one way to ensure God's favour, to explain the injustice of Simeon's suffering. It was the most costly of gifts, befitting only the most important of requests, but to Elijah there was no nobler need in all the world.

THE scout bowed low, first to his sovereign, and then to the council. His weathered hands clapped piercingly and a plant was brought forth. Fragrant drops of nectar clung to its well-nourished buds, causing them to glisten in the sunlight.

"A gift for Your Majesty," said the scout, "from a land where the water still flows."

"Our land has not borne so rich a green in many years," remarked the king.

"It comes from the far east," offered the scout, "through the mountains, east of your eastern encampment."

"I had not been told there was an eastern pass," said the king.

"Scouts have died in the search," said a general.

"They are impassable," said another.

"The path is difficult," admitted the scout, "but I have been through the mountains, and there I have seen a land lush with agriculture. Your eastern army protects Edom from invasion by the north-leading pass. I know the northern peoples, yet at the camp I saw merchants whom I did not recognize. I followed them in secret for many days through mountain trails and caves. When I emerged, I stood above a well-populated land, filled with forests and crops. It is a land of ingenious irrigation. They have directed mountain waters into their fields, so that they no longer rely upon the rain, subject to its seasons."

"What of the people's strength?" asked the first general.

"They number in the thousands, but they are mostly farmers. I could spot no military men amongst them."

"Armies do not easily travel small mountain paths," said the second.

"It is narrow, but sure footed, my Lord."

The king arose, lifting the plant from the table. He carried it toward the window and examined the light gold veins that marked its leaves. Water fell from its buds and landed before the feet of the king.

"My people are saved," he said. "Our salvation lies in the east."

"WELCOME, Eli," said Zechariah, knocking on the open door of the novice's cell. "It is good to see you with us. You were looking for me?"

It was evening, and a single candle lit the room. Shadows danced on the walls under the influence of a draft. Elijah sat on a wooden chair, struggling to read Scripture amidst the changing light. He looked up from the text and replied to the old priest.

"Yes, Father. I've received troubling news from Simeon. His wife is with child, but the physicians fear a stillbirth."

"I am sorry," said Zechariah. "I will pray for them."

The novice paused, composing his words with care. "I've considered the matter, and in response I wish to request my ascension. I'm confident God's favour will be granted; I need only approach."

"No, Elijah," said Father Zechariah, shaking his head with compassion. "The whole of our Order will raise voice to God in prayer on your behalf, but we cannot accept your sacrifice for this matter."

"Won't you take my request before the elders?"

"They will not permit it. I will not permit it."

"Father, I must do this. It's the child's only hope," pleaded Elijah.

"You do not know that, and we do not make this sacrifice lightly. We lay down our lives to end famines, or win wars. We simply cannot die for every cause; we are too few. Your sorrow is terrible, Elijah, and it pains me that you must endure it, but one child's life is not enough. At best we lose one good soul and replace it with another. Therein we do not benefit."

"It's my life, Father. Can't I spend it, if I so see fit?"

"You have only the life that was given you, Eli. Remember that you, in turn, already gave your life to be of service to God under the guidance of this Order."

"I wish only to give that gift of life to another. One good soul can shift the balance of the world. Please, bring my request before the elders."

"The child could also be the source of much wrongdoing; we simply cannot know, Eli. I look upon your brother as a son. He is a good man, generous and honest, amongst the most noble of our land. This, however, holds no guarantees regarding his child. Perhaps it is for the best that these things come to pass."

The elder looked at Elijah and, letting a great sigh leave his lips, he recanted, "Very well, Eli, I will bring the request before the council on your behalf. If the other elders will endorse it, I will not stand in your way."

"Thank you, Father. That's all I can ask."

"Do not thank me, for whatever we decide, it will be with a heavy heart. Our discussion will take some time. While you wait, fast and pray against the need for such drastic action."

Father Zechariah left without further words, and Elijah was alone once more. He returned to the Scriptures, but its text was shrouded by the moving interplay of light and dark that illuminated his cell. Elijah forcefully closed the book in frustration, and blew out the candle.

"T HE harvest feast approaches," said the king. "The discontent of my people may turn their gathering towards revolt. We must feed my people well."

"We must move quickly," said a general.

"Let us send a delegation east at once," suggested a second, who held the eastern watch.

"They are an unknown people, of unknown ways," said the king. "Even the friends of a beggar are soon scattered, and you would introduce us in our need? No, we will not seek conversation, but by our strength we will extract the needs of my people."

"Our armies are strong," agreed the first general.

"We should not attack," countered the other.

"What threat are these farmers to our steel?" asked the king, taken aback by the disunion. "Will their food not feed our people?"

"They are no threat, and they are well fed," replied the general. "My armies rightly defend against the savage north. I will not have them reduced to thieves, brutishly taking what has not been given them. The easterners are not our enemies. There is no need to attack."

"You know of these people," said the king with measure, "and you know of our hunger. If I must choose between the starvation of my people and the blood of these strangers, I will provide for my people. We *will* attack to the east."

"I will not so lead my armies," responded the general.

"Then you will command them no longer," said the king with growing impatience. "Guards! Arrest the general."

"Your Highness," said another general, "he will starve in our prison."

"No lesser punishment would befit such treason," said the king. "He was content for my people to starve, so let him provide them with one more meal. Guards!"

The eastern general maintained a noble stance as the guards surrounded him, amidst the silence of his contemporaries.

"Curse you," he said, "for you have brought a curse upon us all."

ELIJAH waited among the orchards and gardens of the monastery while the elders slowly sought consensus. He remained at peace as the days passed, his apprehension subdued by the past works of his hands. The plants spoke a testament to his life. Their seed had grown where he had nurtured them, and the sound of the wind rustling through their leaves would remain long after he was gone.

It was the morning of the third day when Father Zechariah entered, looking worn from debate. Elijah approached expectantly, but Zechariah only shook his head in response.

"It's not right," said Elijah before the priest could speak.

"Do not lecture me on right and wrong, Elijah. You are still the novice, and I, the priest. God alone can see purpose in the death of Simeon's child, but we cannot give our blessing to your request. As I promised, we will all fast and pray on your behalf."

"Yes, Father," said Elijah.

"The child may not die, Eli," the priest said with a softer tone. "This we do not know. Yet whatever the babe's fate, we must trust in God and have faith in His ways."

"Of course, Father."

Zechariah looked on Elijah with concern.

"We are not all called to ascend," he said, "and rarely at a time of our own choosing. In my younger days, I might have felt otherwise. Yet as I look back upon the years, I am thankful for the parts I have played among the living. Consider the Garden of St. Enoch. It is an important work. The time may come for your calling, but, until that day, trust that your life is well spent."

"I will return to the garden," said Elijah, "that I may continue my good deed."

"So soon?" said Zechariah. "Will you not pray and fast among us?"

"My soul yearns for solitude, Father. In the stillness of the garden I can best reflect on the council's ruling."

"Please understand our decision," said the priest. "We cannot right every wrong on this earth, no matter our desire, and we must use reason to balance the weight of our convictions. Faith leads us, but reason must also support our deeds."

"Does reason nurture our faith?" asked Elijah. "I find that hard to believe. It seems to me that we betray our faith when we seek to justify its direction."

"And yet we act in folly when we ignore the guidance of reason," said Zechariah. "There are times when we must follow our conscience at the expense of reason, but it is wisdom that guides us on the right course between our knowledge and our heart. In this I pray we have succeeded."

"As do I, Father," said Elijah, quieter than before. "I do not wish to depart with harsh words between us, but I must be going. I'd like to reach Simeon before nightfall. Thank you, Father, for bringing my request to the council. You've given much to Simeon and me. I am always grateful."

"You and your brother have also been a blessing to me, and I am proud of you both. You speak with wisdom, Eli, and your words bear truth, but also hear the veracity of my convictions and consider them during your travels. May God watch over you and may St. Enoch act as your guide. Give your brother my greeting."

"I will, Father," said Elijah.

After watching the old priest return to the monastery, Elijah went on, "I must continue in faith, with or without the council's blessing. I'll miss you, Father Zechariah, but as you have said so often, I must do what I can with what I've been given. I pray you'll forgive me in time."

IT was dark when Elijah neared his brother's home, his path illuminated by the moon above. On approach, he could see the fire-given light that escaped the small hut. It radiated, at a distance, a peaceful warmth welcomed by the novice, but his heart was torn between its lambent glow and the surrounding shadow of night, the disquiet of his soul.

"What can I say?" he wondered, looking at the hut. "The right path is before me, but Simeon won't understand. No, my request must remain secret. I cannot speak of these things."

As he drew closer, Elijah became immersed in the familiar sounds of Simeon's life. Sheep bleated softly, penned in the darkness. The crunch of the path beneath his feet gave way to the crinkle of fallen leaves, whose branches stood bare along the parched pathway. The creak of steps and the sounds of tender voices.

Elijah paused, savouring the serenity of a blessed home.

His arrival was greeted with joy. Tabitha hugged him warmly, while Simeon stood, smiling broadly.

"Little brother!" he said. "It's good to see you. You're returning south so soon?"

"Enoch's garden calls," said Elijah, "and so I go."

"Have you eaten?" asked Tabitha. "Would you like some bread?"

They shared a meal at a modest table, in the heat and light of the crackling fire. With the taste of bread and sour wine still lingering in their mouths, they discussed the impacts of the drought, the people's hunger and unrest. They spoke of sheep and wool, pastures and dyes, until Elijah could no longer avoid the question that plagued his mind.

"Has there been any movement?" he asked bluntly.

Tabitha was quiet. She moved her hand over her belly, as if hopeful for some sign of life.

"It is both a mystery and a certainty," she said at length, "but God is aware of our suffering. I do not know why He allows His children to suffer, but who can know the mind of God? Or can it be that, in the name of some greater good, He causes our discomfort, relying on our faith to endure? Are we blessed in suffering, that God has faith in our strength to abide these trials? He who is the source of all confidence now calls upon us to use it. We will not be tested beyond what we can bear."

"Upon such faith is built the kingdom of heaven," said Elijah, making the sign of St. Enoch, "but the injustices of the world demand a response, and your child's death is most certainly the highest injustice."

"I will weep if our child dies," said Tabitha, "and if I die, others will weep for me. We live according to the will of God."

Afterwards, Simeon and Elijah stood in silence under the stars. Elijah had been shaken by Tabitha's words, a feeling quite unknown to him. Little had been spoken since her response. Words of conviction and truth, Simeon had said, often gave birth to contemplation.

"What is the right response to our trials?" Elijah asked, giving voice to his doubts.

"We bring our requests to God in prayer," said Simeon. "Sometimes a faithful endurance is all that's required."

Simeon's words gave Elijah no comfort and, later that night, he felt ashamed as he sat alone staring at the last glowing embers of the fire. The foundation of his Order torn asunder: the gift of one's life rendered foolish in the light of faithful communion on earth. For if God's ear were ever so close, why approach Him in death?

As if in answer to his question, Elijah heard Tabitha's suffering in the night. Quietly at first, muffled by pillows and self-control, Elijah heard her weep, the evening's brave words overcome by the realities of darkness. To his listening ear, each broken sob returned justice to his Order's calling.

The darkness passed by morning and Tabitha, composed once more, hugged Elijah strongly, bidding him safety in his travels. Elijah, too, felt renewed courage for his journey.

"Isn't it lonely in the garden?" asked Simeon.

"I won't be in the garden long this time," said Elijah. "May Enoch bring you peace, brother. You'll never be far from me."

Elijah untied two great packs of food from his mule and carried them over to his brother.

"It's too much," he protested. "What will you eat?"

"All that I need is already in the garden," said Elijah.

Tabitha brought forward a wool blanket.

"It can be cold at night, even in the Garden of St. Enoch," she said. "It will keep you warm."

"It will," said Elijah, "both in body and spirit. Thank you."

THE drought had challenged the royal garden, but its maintenance had been achieved, and achieved well. Their chief attendant stood in the court of the king, summoned to the company of his council.

"The cultivation of a garden is a slow process, Your Highness," he explained with pride, "whose works pass from one generation to the next, yet the works of a single season can dramatically change its face forever. What we have done here will be remembered for generations to come. Our garden is green, even without the rain."

"You have done well," said the king. "Your work is a service to all of Edom, and its garden has grown even in the most difficult of times. My people have suffered this past year and need reprieve. They need to see the strength of their kingdom, a strength made clear by the harvest feast, and the venue you have maintained."

"No one who sees the splendour of our garden could question Edom's strength, Your Highness," said the attendant, "its endurance through this present hardship. Prized specimens, birds and plants, have been imported from all the known world. They flower and sing to your glory, O King."

"To the glory of Edom," corrected the king. "This is to be a feast worthy of legend. You have provided a venue worthy of such exclaim and bear the thankfulness of the whole kingdom."

"It is my honour, my Lord."

"I have one more flower to add," said the king, motioning for the gold-veined plant to be brought forth. A massive flower of deepest crimson now adorned its crown.

"I have never seen such beauty," said the gardener. "From where did it come?"

"A gift from God," he said. "It brings hope for our kingdom. Its flower is the promise of salvation."

"It will have a place of highest honour."

The gardener lifted the plant with awe. The smell of its sweet nectar filled the air.

"You are dismissed," said the king.

The attendant bowed low. As he departed, the king turned to his council.

"How go preparations for our meal?" he asked.

"Our troops will soon attack," said a general.

"May their victory be swift," said the king, "else our garden is but a vanity."

"HE who gave us all confidence now calls upon us to use it," echoed Elijah, stepping from the Tomb onto the ancient soil of St. Enoch's garden. From high above, a full moon illuminated the land in a transparent white. The wind blew, and the leaves moved.

He had been in prayer since late afternoon, seeking guidance at the king's feet. With thankfulness and confession, he spoke to God and, receiving no sign to the contrary, felt the direction of a greater will as he collected water from around the sarcophagus of St. Enoch.

Elijah set the water to boil atop a fire. He collected hemlock leaves and generously added them to steep. A musty fragrance filled his nose as the hot liquid drew the poison from the plant.

He removed a satin cloth from his satchel as he waited. Layer by layer he unfolded it until, at its core, he withdrew the scratched pewter cup he had drawn from the worn statue's base. With sober judgment, he inspected its dented exterior and felt its cold weight in his hand.

"I will drink of death," he said, "that God may hear their cry."

Parchment and quill, he took from his satchel. "Let the child live," he said, giving voice to the words as he wrote them. Rolled and sealed, he tied them over his shoulder and across his chest.

Elijah filled his cup with the steaming brew and extinguished the fire with what remained. He looked to the stars as it cooled, and spoke to the heavens in practiced verse:

Through dark of death, we pass away:
This loss of life, our noblest deed.
God's righteous will, we ask to sway:
His ear we bend, in greatest need.

The sufferings of this world seek voice:
it pains our heart, our souls compel.
Though we will die, we will rejoice.
For by this gift, we sins dispel.

With the closing of his prayer, Elijah reverently raised his drink to the place where Enoch lay.

"For the weeping faithful," he said. "Hear our cry."

Elijah drank deeply of the cup and climbed the stage amidst a growing wind. He surveyed the garden with failing eyes. The smoldering fire was distant. He felt cold. Elijah drew Tabitha's blanket around him. The memory of its warmth brought comfort, peace and purpose.

"Soon I will see my God," Elijah said in fading voice. "Soon I will stand in His glory."

Elijah propped himself against a pillar, his hand growing numb as it lamely brushed the rough canister tied over his heart. Strength left his hands and feet. Death crept through his veins. His body grew limp, and the wind stopped, silent.

"INSUFFERABLE," muttered Obadiah. still unsettled at three hours past midnight. Searching the palace halls for sleep, he found another who was given no rest. The old priest wished to carry on unnoticed, but the king's tired voice called out after him.

"How rare it is to see you at this late hour," said the monarch.

"Even a man of faith has the occasion for sleepless nights," said Obadiah. "We all wrestle with the world's injustice. What robs you of your rest tonight, Highness?"

"At last I have had a dream, priest. I was an assassin, waiting atop the palace walls with bow drawn. When my mark came forth, I was taken aback, for it was myself. I was both the archer and the target."

"Did you loose your arrow?" wondered Obadiah aloud.

"I awoke from the image," said the king, "but it plagues my mind. There is a shadow over my people. The light is denied them, blocked by an unseen assailant, and my light alone is but too dim. Two candles burn brighter together. The queen's light is now so far away, and we all live in darkness."

"The queen is mourned by us all, Your Highness," said Obadiah, noticing Hannah's copper-cased compass in the king's hand, "but the body needs rest, and errors are often made by an exhausted mind."

"We know that the rains come and the crops grow, but is water truly what we lack?" said the king. "Of what are we ever certain, priest? It is all conjecture. We know what we are told, and we know what we see, yet our eyes can be deceived, and our instruction is oft filled with untruth. With these as our guides must we prepare for the future? With this corrupt reason must we diagnose the present?"

"Queen Hannah once told me that we all must trust in something," recalled the priest. "We all must apply some measure to connect the events of our lives. She did not fear the mistakes that would be made, the misleadings of false conceptions, but rather she was comforted that true meaning is founded on many footings. Have faith that God will guide, even with a broken compass."

"Reason is a religion with no God."

"And yet God is not without reason, Your Highness. Though His purposes may be beyond our comprehension, I *am* certain they are not arbitrary. The queen once reflected how often we confuse the foundation of life with its edifices. God does not stand on reason, but reason stands on the order of God. Faith stands on His constancy, but its footing is the same. Queen Hannah went so far as to insist that the relentless pursuit of reason was the death of the heart, while the rigid pursuit of faith was the death of the mind. While both are gifts of God, neither can reveal Him in isolation. God is neither faith nor reason, that we could so define Him. In mystery, He responds to us by His character. So let our deeds reflect His wisdom, and let us not be limited in our understanding."

"Thank you for your council," said the king, "but the fish cannot fly any more than the bird can swim. I am bound to what I see, and I do not see God's hand in our plight. God may be in His heavens, but we are on this earth."

"Even the greatest king is but a steward, my Lord, entrusted to fulfill the noblest hopes of man to the glory of God."

"Good night, priest," said the king. "Know that I, too, have acted for the hopes of my people. Their suffering and sacrifice have always been towards their good end."

A turning of sky above breathless sand, another soul plummets. Sockets.

Sockets without eyes, watching.

Watching from the sand. Watching is the sand.

The feel of stone. The texture of wood. Insatiable desire. Echoes torn asunder.

Terror. Elijah stood atop the stage. Millions of arms reaching, touching, wrenching. Figures rising from the sand, fighting over the shadows of his life. The abrasive grip of a million yearning souls reducing his garden to dust. Forms of sand surround him. Statue, stage and lectern erode into the desert under the immeasurable coveting of the dead.

Fear. Not of death, but of life lost. Elijah wrenched a small stone back from the sand: a pebble from an island in the ocean of death. The sand fought back. Its desire was no greater. It did not overcome. The sand turned to the other remnants of his life.

Sorrow. Elijah fell to his knees and wept, the echoes of his past life eroding around him, the strength of rock crumbling to ruin amidst his falling tears.

The sand grew still, and Elijah was alone.

Forming a cup of his clenched hands, Elijah found that he, as the sand, had coveted too much. His stone, the last vestige of his life, had been reduced to dust.

Echoes no more. A wail. A moan. A whimper.

Prostrate on the sand, coarse grains shifting surround him. Searing heat. Freezing cold. Cloth. A corner exposed. Tabitha's blanket, tattered. Gently drawn from the desert.

Elijah rose. He wrapped the blanket, holey and faded, about his shoulders. Lifting his eyes from the sand below, he looked to the sky above. Sand there, too. An unbroken stratus of sand. Sand below and sand above.

The weight of dunes rise about him. Mountains of sand obscure the desert. Mountains of sand are the desert. A path through the mountains. A dune made flat. A mountain, fallen. Elijah walks.

THE arms of sand lay still, a soul alone. But not alone. Elijah could see him, standing among the dust, a great staff in his hand. Close now. Distant. Elijah called out. He turned and was near.

"Hello," said Elijah.

A nod of head. Silence.

"I'm not alone," said Elijah.

Eyebrow raised. "It is a vast desert," said the stranger. "We are always and never alone."

Tarnished reflection in the sand. Elijah knelt down, retrieved, stood. Reflection in hand. A sound out of place. Crowing. Laughter. Muted by the sand.

"Why do you laugh?" asked Elijah. Disbelief.

"The queen's broken compass," said the stranger, looking to Elijah's hand. "It finds me even in death."

"It's not broken," said Elijah. "See, the needle turns."

The stranger looked. Surprise.

"What does this mean?" he asked. "Who are you?"

"I am Elijah, of St. Enoch."

"I am King Enoch."

"Praise God!" exclaimed the novice, kneeling at the king's feet. "Enoch himself is my guide."

"I have only a staff," said the king, "but you hold my compass."

"We'll walk together," said Elijah. "To the east, the birthplace of light, for surely there we'll find our way from this unholy land. Together we will reach God."

The king watched the sand that surrounded them. It shifted left and right, without destination and without direction. He turned to the novice.

"To the east," he said.

"OUR army is defeated?" asked the king in disbelief.

"Yes, Your Highness," said the messenger, with downcast eyes.

"How did this happen?" demanded the king.

"Their former general is suspect," said the messenger. "On the night we were to raid, an army rose from within our own ranks. We were slaughtered without defence."

"What of the defectors?" asked the king.

"They have allied themselves with our adversary and dwell among them."

The king paused at this report. The food stores were empty, and the feast was tomorrow. His people were hungry. His people were angry. *'They will revolt,'* he thought with certainty. *'By their anger, we will be undone. Was it all for naught?'*

"Is the former general still alive?" the king asked.

"Yes, Your Majesty," said a general.

"Give him what food you can and clothe him," said the king. "Restore his status and set him free. Set all the prisoners free. The blood of others will no longer be on my hands."

"My Lord?"

"You have heard my orders," he said. "Now leave me. All of you, be gone!"

Obadiah stayed at the side entry as the last general left the hall. He watched with fear and pity, unseen by the king, as the monarch paced before his own thrown, speaking to himself.

"Have I been deceived?" he asked aloud. "What falsehood seen, what lies heard, that our course ends in death? Yet if all for naught, such needless suffering have I caused. Many, so many, have I sacrificed towards this end. How many more would satisfy? Perhaps only one is needed."

The monarch turned and noticed Obadiah. He said nothing, however, and walked quickly from the room. The priest called after him, but the king paid him no heed.

S AND flowing, they stumbled. Sand burning, they bled. Mountains rose. Mountains fell. And the needle turned.

Stumbling. Falling. Kneeling. Crawling. Enoch and Elijah followed. And the needle turned.

"Leave your staff," said Elijah. "It weighs you down."

"I will not," said the king. "It supports me still."

Thirsting. Burning. Parching. Yearning. A thirst of the soul, a burden of the spirit.

"I see water," said Enoch.

There was a pool in the distance with a tree by its waters. With hope they pressed on: the water, a drink to their spirit; the tree, a shade for their soul.

"The needle points away," said Elijah.

"Should we not act according to what sight we are given?" asked Enoch.

They looked to the water and were thirsty. The promise of renewal, the prospect of peace: a step towards the pool. Still the needle pointed away.

"It's not right," said Elijah.

"We will wash our feet in its waters," said Enoch, "and be quenched by its spring."

So they went to the waters; they walked to the tree.

"There's no shade here," observed Elijah as they neared. "The tree is dead, its leaves lost long ago."

Enoch continued to the pool and placed his foot beneath its still surface. Blisters formed where its waters touched. Pulling sharply back, the king returned to Elijah. He limped slightly as he walked, relying on his staff to bear him.

"It is caustic," he said, "and provides no comfort. Let us continue as the compass leads."

Weary. To the desert they returned.

"Our sin was not to follow our eyes," said Elijah. "We denied the compass. We mustn't let our minds overcome the burden of our conscience."

"SIMEON, Tabitha, please understand," pleaded Isaac, the physician. "Each month I come, and each month it is the same. Your belly has hardly grown, your womb shows no movement, and your child gives no heartbeat. Your child *is* dead, and Tabitha's life is jeopardized without cause. Do not compound this tragedy."

"We cannot live in the uncertainty that we may have killed our only child," said Simeon. "We wait in the hope that our facts will be turned

into folly. If there is a stillbirth, that is God's decision, but I won't have our babe's blood on my hands."

"Then you will have your wife's blood also," said the physician. "I can assure you that any healthy pregnancy exhibits some sign of life. Your child shows none, and it *is* dead. Let me induce labour, let me save Tabitha."

"No," said Tabitha firmly.

"Then I can do nothing," said the physician sadly. "Send for me if you change your mind, else I will not come this way again."

E LIJAH and Enoch continued further into the desert. Their speed was slowed by the gait of the king, who now leaned heavily on his staff, causing it to sink into the sand. Elijah pushed on, eyes never lifting from the compass.

"The compass points the way," said Elijah. "Ours is simply to follow, and in obedience we will be saved."

The ground was growing soft, however, and Elijah's steps began to sink beneath its surface. The sand stuck to his legs and weighed down his feet. Enoch slowed further.

"The ground grows weak," he said. "We cannot go that way."

"We're following the compass," said Elijah, sinking deeper. "All else is distraction."

Enoch followed no further. He pushed his staff into the sand and tested the steps before him.

"Do you think yourself equal to the angels?" he called out, further now from Elijah. "Only those who are carried on the wind need not consider the strength of the ground beneath their feet."

But Elijah pressed on, and the dust engulfed him. Its arms reached out. Its hands touched and tore. An encroachment of sand. The becoming of sand. It clung to his skin and shallowed his breath. It blocked the light. It left him in darkness.

Thoughts slowed.

Sentence became phrase.

Phrase, fragment.

A soul.

Asunder.

A staff.

A reaching hand.

The thought that had been Elijah was ripped from the void, wrenched back from the desert that claimed him and cast down atop the sand.

"We cannot so follow," said the king, standing tall. "The compass may give direction, but we are bound to this earth and, though east lies our destination, we must walk on ground that will bear us. See! We are too heavy for so straight a path. We cannot fly even as birds, let alone angels. But there are stones that would bear us, hidden beneath the sand. The prod of my staff can reveal them. Meandering is their course, but their strength is true."

Elijah wept.

"Will we deny the compass?" he said quietly.

"Our bearing will be set by its hand," assured Enoch, "but to follow the staff need not mean denial. Indeed, the staff is our guide when the needle points where we simply cannot go. Follow the path my burden reveals, else we will be lost to the sand."

Elijah arose and followed. He trailed as Enoch led them slowly through the desert, his heart sinking as they strayed further from the needle's course. His spirit lifted, however, as they in time turned true, and he praised God with new understanding for both the compass and the staff.

The dust was subdued once more; watching and wailing from a distance. Though painful and wandering was their path, Enoch and Elijah went east.

WITH apprehension Father Zechariah stood before the small house. The soft bleating of sheep, penned for the night, fell silent with his approach. Zechariah paused again, his stare fixed upon the door. Drawing a breath, he knocked. Simeon answered.

"Father Zechariah!" he said with hushed pleasure. He stepped out, closing the door behind. "Tabitha is resting." he explained.

"Eli spoke of her condition," said Zechariah. "We are all praying for her."

"Thank you, Father," said Simeon. "It's good to see you."

Then Simeon paused. He noticed the weary lines that painted sorrow on Zechariah's face, He saw the pained look in the old priest's eyes. "What brings you here so late?" he said, concerned. "Is Eli alright?"

"I am afraid not," said Zechariah. "Prayer was not enough for him."

"What do you mean?" asked Simeon.

"He believed that he must seek God more directly," said Zechariah. "He has Ascended on your behalf."

"He's dead?" asked Simeon.

"He is," said Zechariah, "for the love of you and your family."

Simeon was silent. Anger grew within him, but it could not overcome the love that he still held for his brother.

"My humble and prideful brother!" he said, calling to the heavens. "Why have you left me?"

"Forgive me, Father Zechariah," he said, aware of the priest before him. "You have been as a parent to us both. Your love of Eli was evident to all. We have both lost family. Tell me, why was this ordained? Why wasn't I told? I would not have allowed it."

Zechariah paused. "It was against our command," he explained. "Eli acted alone, without our blessing."

"Will he be able to reach God if he chose to defy the will of the elders?" asked Simeon. "Will the elders choose to bless Eli's act, and pray that he reaches God?"

"This is a good and difficult question," Zechariah responded. "It is not simple to answer. Elijah chose to defy our council, which we believe to be true. St. Hannah once wrote that free will was the greatest gift bestowed to God's creation, for only a free spirit can truly commune with Him. But it was also the most costly of His gifts, for all this world's calamities are drawn from a will other than our Lord's.

"Eli chose to give his life. Will we choose to deny our wisdom and call his act blessed? I do not know. In time, perhaps. Blessed or not, I do pray that Eli's act will lead him into communion with God."

"Thank you, Father," said Simeon. "The night is long, and I grow weary. Will you stay with us?"

"Not this night," said Zechariah. "I wish to walk further, that the air may clear my mind. You will all be in my prayers."

Simeon returned to his home, and Zechariah was, once again, alone on the path to the mountain. The old priest extinguished his torch, and walked several miles by the dim light of the crescent moon. Worn and exhausted, he fell onto his knees and tore his cloak.

"*How long? How long? How long?*" he cried to the heavens,

How long will our prayers be in vain?
How long will You be silent?
Your children fall before you.
Are our deaths worth more than our lives?
Answer, oh God, and do not be silent.

But You alone are God.
I am a twig, consumed in Your fire.
You alone send the rain.
I am a leaf, carried on Your wind.
You alone give us breath.
I am a stem, upheld by Your root.
You alone are my support.
Who can fathom the ways of God?

CENTURIES earlier, King Enoch knelt in a similar pose overlooking his kingdom. As his gaze moved to the heavens above, he spread his arms and also cried to God in a loud voice:

You appoint Your kings and hold them to account.
You herald their authority,
and their governance You uphold.

Yet by what compass shall they steer?
Is there no star that points us true?
No steadfast wind that blows us right?

You are concealed by the world,
and shrouded behind the vision of our eyes.
Still we suffer Your displeasure.

Open your mouth and speak against us.
Make your charge, and I will answer.
For You have hidden the righteous path.

Your ways are not my ways,
but Your people are my people.
Thus two rulers cannot reign.

I will no longer be held responsible.
Their cries I cannot silence,
and their wounds I cannot heal.

For you alone are God.
Against such might, who can stand?
But I, too, will demand an accounting.

In death I will see Your face.
In passing will I stand before You.
Our suffering tale will reach Your ear.

And so I come.
I come.
I come.

THE king and the novice came to a great boulder on the eastern desert plain. It stood tall before them, and its shadow cooled their skin. The weary pair rested against its dark face and looked back at the sand. The sand watched them intently; its voice was silent.

"Can the desert become fertile?" asked Elijah, with growing clarity. "Or is each grain forever dry? It is a vast desert."

"We are sand," admitted the king, "washed neither by the rain above nor the springs below."

"Yet even here there is grace," said Elijah, holding the compass firmly. "If we seek to act rightly and but trust in God, using the gifts He has given, we will be saved. He is God, and we, man."

"There is no redemption in the desert," said Enoch. "My life has passed. By the staff I ruled, and by the staff I am rightly judged."

"Great King," said Elijah, "your deeds are known and praised throughout all of Edom. Surely their songs have been lifted even to the ear of God. What do you have to fear?"

"But few of my deeds were great," said Enoch. "I merely followed the reasonable course, but it could not save us."

"Your works were worthy of legend," insisted Elijah. "You were the greatest of us. Famine threatened our land in a time long past. You sacrificed your very life to plead before God, that He might show mercy. God was pleased, and with your death the rains returned. Edom was saved, and you were our saviour."

"I died, and the rains came," said the king pensively. "A time long past in life: a moment and an eternity in death."

"We follow the path you set before us," continued Elijah, "pleading with God for the mercy of others."

"The legend of my life is not its truth," said the king. "If the rains came at my death, it was not because I had pleased God. My life was not of such merit."

A crack appeared at the base of the rock. It spread up the boulder's smooth surface and widened to produce a small, cool stream. Water poured onto the desert sand and covered the travellers' feet. They knelt and drank, lifting water to their mouths and pouring it over their heads. They rose and, in wonder, watched the compass needle as it turned to the rock. The crevice grew and gave entrance to the darkness.

Stepping through the water, the pair entered.

S ILENCE followed the king's prayer.

"Your Highness!" shouted Obadiah, banging on the king's locked door.

Gideon approached, and both priests exchanged a knowing glance.

"Damn him," said the old priest. "In death he will cause more destruction than in life. Only by the terror of the king's retribution have riots been withheld. Once his death is known, they will storm the palace. There is no heir, no ruler in Edom."

"Then we are lost," agreed Gideon. "The feast is tomorrow night; we cannot hide the king's death. With neither food nor king, the people will seek answers."

For a time, both men remained silent, standing at the king's doorstep. It was late, and their minds were muddled by exhaustion.

It was Gideon who spoke: "There is nothing to do but alert the generals. Perhaps they can bring peace."

"Not tonight," said Obadiah. "Grant me this evening."

"As you wish," said Gideon, hesitantly.

Obadiah shook his head, as if answering some unspoken question, and granted Gideon leave. The shadows deepened as he moved away, until his lamp faded from sight, leaving the old priest in darkness.

"Damn," muttered Obadiah again under his breath.

Stumbling into the courtyard, Obadiah found himself among the festival's nearly complete preparations. In the moonlight he could see thousands of tables set out for the anticipated feast. The people were hungry, and the promise of food would draw together the entire kingdom.

The king was no fool. Starving and angry, the people's rage would demand blood. Death would have come to the king soon, whether or not by his own hand.

"Are we to accept that which we hold inevitable?" asked Obadiah. "Is a lesser, but sure, evil more right?"

A vastness beyond measure, encased in a stone. Starlight shimmered off the water that bathed Enoch and Elijah's feet. They walked on the smoothness of soapstone, whose cool surface was as balm to their sores.

Oblique walls obstructed their view on either side. They looked ahead to where the walls ended, to where a fountain cast its water towards heaven. The sound of its falling droplets mixed with angelic voices above. Harmonious tones blended with the rain, bathed in a golden light, redirected from some distant source.

Enoch and Elijah walked towards the fountain. Its mist grew thick, and they could see nothing but the growing intensity of light. Droplets clung to their skin and washed their soiled clothing. Parched lips became moist. Broken spirits became whole.

Passing through the waters, they saw a great walled city. Its light poured heavenward, illuminating a host of winged creatures that encircled it from above. Theirs was the song of heaven, the exaltation of their King.

An abyss cut deep into the earth between the travellers and the city walls. Its expanse was breached by a bridge, narrowly formed from the stone. Chiselled tears fell from the massive sculpture of a man who embraced the archway, the opening of which allowed entrance to a distant light. His eyes looked deeply at the novice, and Elijah knew his tears as those that fell a lifetime away, outside the tomb of St. Hannah. The faint sound of feasting blended with the angelic chorus and carried across the chasm, inviting Enoch and Elijah forward, beseeching them to join in their praise.

Refreshed though they felt, the king's limp remained, and with a sinking heart he beheld the bridge before them. Enoch sat at the water's edge, his staff held tightly in his hand. He looked to the city and again to the bridge. Elijah sat beside him.

"It is too narrow to walk with a staff," said the king.

He listened to the music for a time, and then the king, in his still-tattered robes, knelt down by the pool. He again lifted its shimmering water to his lips and drank.

He sat once more and spoke quietly, "In life, many horrible deeds were done at my hand. I ordered deaths and starvations, raised wars and pillaged. Yet even here, in the presence of this heavenly kingdom, I am still convinced of their necessity. Some evils are committed to prevent even greater atrocities. There are but few of my deeds that would I change."

"There is righteous reason," said Elijah, "of which God will not condemn. I've seen it in the desert, and I've praised Him for its guidance, but grace is greater still. It shields us from His right judgment, when our reason and our desire have led us astray."

"But I did not go astray," said Enoch. "God may not be pleased when righteousness gives way to reason, yet my very substance has fixed its faith therein. I have neither the strength nor the will to overcome. I had no other guide, no truer voice to counsel me."

"All may be redeemed," insisted Elijah.

"My life is complete," said Enoch. "I seek no redemption, for I committed no crime."

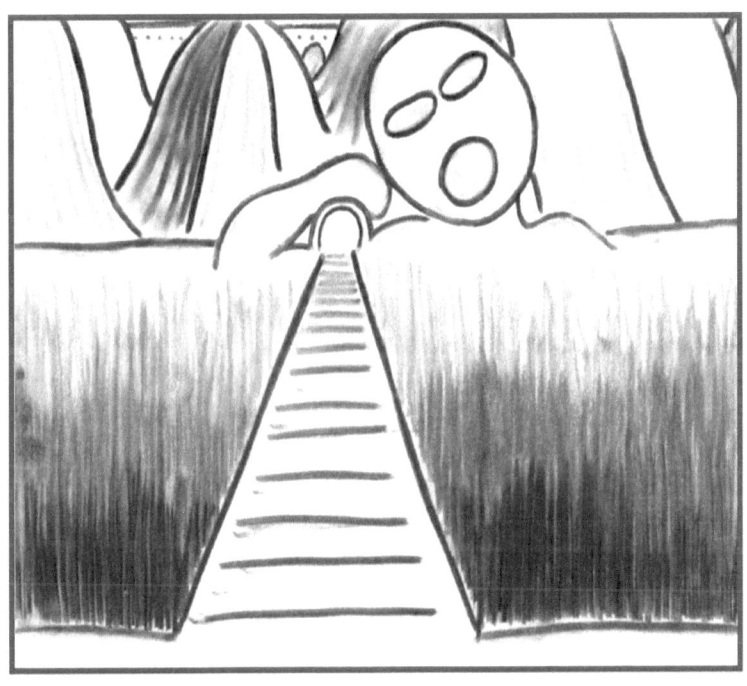

"Even the great are not worthy, but by God's grace they may enter His kingdom. The thankful heart may approach."

"You did not listen," said the king. "God's judgment may not rest on reason, but by that staff I ruled, and by its way would I be rightly judged. I would rather sit here, sheltered by the rock, yet shielded from His judgment against which I can make no defence."

"What is this rock save the grace of God? If you are to be judged, you will be judged. Only His mercy can save you, whether sheltered by this rock or burning in the desert. Let us cross the bridge together and seek His pardon."

The king considered his words and said, "I will cross, but still I will not ask for mercy, only a righteous judgment. I will offer my life and enter in, if God so deems it worthy."

PUSHED outside his home by the midwives' charge, Simeon paced with fervor.

His wife's first cry brought him terror, and the following silence, torment.

Tabitha's second and third painful cries filled the air. Simeon took each cycle with increased agony until, filled with grief, he fell to the ground and wept.

OBADIAH awoke to the rumble of thunder. His wondering eyes met with storm clouds set alight from the flashes within. The old priest had fallen asleep in the garden, and with his face still etched from slumber, he felt the first raindrop slide across his skin. One became many, and the water washed over him.

The rain brought understanding. Obadiah saw. He saw a king's faithless rule, the pride of unchecked reason. He saw rain withheld from the earth. But God had not forgotten them: there was a path to his people's redemption.

When Gideon joined him in the garden, Obadiah was staring up at the sky, the rain pouring down.

"It is glorious, isn't it?" said Gideon.

Obadiah smiled in response.

"I have missed it," said Gideon, "but we have no time for such pleasures."

The old priest still said nothing.

"The people will soon arrive for the feast," pressed Gideon. "What shall we do?"

"Let them in," said Obadiah.

"We will need the palace gates if they riot," said Gideon. "What will we say of the king?"

"He will show himself, in good time," said Obadiah. "Prepare for the feast."

Baffled, Gideon watched his brother stride toward the garden's edge.

"Do not fear!" Obadiah called. "We have much to celebrate. Everything is obvious, for now I understand!"

B Y early afternoon, the rain had quieted, but not stopped. After so much time in absence, it was welcomed with celebration. The gathered crowd murmured in anticipation; the air filled with the thought of a king's banquet bestowed upon his faithful subjects.

The people watched as a priest slowly made his way to the lectern. Obadiah raised his hand for silence and spoke:

"It is well known that our king and our God did not often see eye to eye. To many of you, our desperate situation is also quite clear. Before today, a drop of rain had not fallen on our land in six months; for years our crops have dwindled. And so, while we are here to celebrate our harvest feast, it is a year in which we have had no harvest and for which we cannot feast.

"Our great king tried everything in his power to provide for us; it was all to no avail. And now, in an effort to save his people, he has given his very life. He has passed beyond the vale of death, that he might plead on our behalf before God Himself.

"I give you our king and our saint, Enoch. He has given us the rain, for the heavens weep with his departure. Let us pay him homage."

Shocked thousands bowed in silence as an ornate coffin was carried forward. In solemn procession, the king's body was carried to the lectern's base and laid at the feet of Father Obadiah.

"Let us always remember and give thanks to our great king. Let us never forget the sacrifice that he has made. May we, in our time, be as willing to sacrifice ourselves in the service of others.

"There are hard times ahead, but we will persevere with St. Enoch, the King of Edom, now at God's side. Amen."

E NOCH looked into the abyss. Blackness silenced the void, and even the angel's music was lost to his ears. The king fixed his gaze upon his companion and walked towards the bridge.

Elijah had already reached its base, and had stopped several paces over the chasm. He did not move, but gazed at his hands. Away from the water, they had grown leprous. With sorrow, he humbly watched his skin dry and crack, blood seeping between his fingers.

"I do not understand," said the king. "If you are so judged, what hope may I sustain?"

"All have sinned," said the novice. "Thought and deed both known and unknown, even those thought noble, can rightly deserve judgment. It is a grace to see our folly. In spite of ourselves we may approach God."

Enoch limped onto the bridge towards him, its narrow width no more than his shoulders. He angled his body slightly and put his staff before him, clenching it with both his hands. As mud baked in the sun, the bridge's stone pealed and broke out from around the staff. The staff itself cracked in two causing the king's hands, also, to bleed, its splinters driven deep within him.

Elijah stood and watched. Beneath his own feet, the stone's smooth black surface remained unchanged. Enoch staggered back to the edge of the abyss and watched the stone mend in his absence.

"I believe here we part," reflected the king.

"Together, we'll reach God," said the novice.

"One cannot reason with stone. I wish you well; may God's mercy shield you and your hope be fulfilled." Bowing gracefully, Enoch turned and limped back towards the pool.

"You can touch me," Elijah called out after him, "and I can touch the bridge. I'll carry you."

Enoch stopped, but did not turn.

"If the bridge begins to crack, we will return and I will cross alone," he continued.

Enoch shook his head, his eyes fixed upon the water.

"I won't let you fall," Elijah insisted.

"You would be judged with me?" said Enoch.

"I would have you know God."

"I do not wish an eternal death," said the king, at length. "We will cross together. But better that you should reach God alone than that we both should be lost."

Enoch climbed onto Elijah's back. Elijah carried him onto the bridge. The ancient traverse groaned in misery. It cracked, but did not break beneath his heavy-laden steps.

Enoch looked to the city ahead and held tightly onto the novice who carried him. It was a long walk over an endless abyss. As the city drew nearer, hope grew within the king.

"We are almost across the bridge!" he said to himself. "Will I, too, know God?"

Rising from the archway with the splintering of stone, the giant sculpture of a man rose before them. Its terrible and sorrowful form blocked their passage. Fire burned in its mouth, and the heat of its breath blew over them, searing their skin and halting their advance.

"You cannot carry him further," it said.

"By my vocation, I can neither leave him, nor let him fall," called Elijah. "I will not abandon him."

"So be it," said the creature, without moving.

Elijah turned his head to see the king.

"Are you near enough to see God?" he asked.

The king looked upon the sculpture before him, wondering at the tears in its eyes. He could see there was light beyond the archway, but the monstrous figure before them trapped them in the shadow of its radiance. The fury of its breath raged over him, and the king quietly responded to the novice with a shake of his head.

"Then may God be merciful," said Elijah, as he took a step forward.

From both sides of the expanse stone began to crumble, falling, black on black, into the void. Enoch abandoned Elijah's back. He watched the bridge deteriorate. He watched it become dust around them.

In their remaining moment, Enoch looked to Elijah. Tears flowed down the novice's face, and Enoch saw the light of heaven glisten brightly off each one.

"Forgive me," said the king, "may my action not be too late."

Then the great King of Edom turned to jump into the abyss, but Elijah firmly grabbed his arm and stayed him. Looking at the failing stone around them, Elijah said only, "May God's will be done."

The bridge faltered.

And they were no more.

I N a near and distant place, rain, much like the rain of the past, began to fall. It fell across the whole of Edom. It poured down from the mountains and drew grass up from the parched earth. It fell on Simeon, still kneeling in the night outside his house, his strained ears searching for Tabitha's pain-filled voice within the ceaseless rush of water.

The door opened, and a baby's cry pierced both water and darkness. A midwife stepped out, light briefly escaping to the night as she shut the door behind her.

"Is Tabitha alright?" demanded Simeon.

"She's fine," assured the midwife.

"And the child?"

"Your new children are quite healthy," she said. "You have twin sons."

"Twins?" asked Simeon. "How can it be? The birth went well?"

"It was complicated," said the midwife. "The first child came out backwards. He did not want to leave his brother behind. He held his brother's arm and pulled him out from the womb."

"But they are fine?" said Simeon. "We were told that there wasn't any movement, no heartbeat."

"Yes, they're fine," said the midwife. "With twins, they may simply not have had the room to move, or perhaps they were asleep."

"I didn't know," said Simeon. "The physician . . . "

" . . . also has limits to his understanding," said the midwife, "as do we all. In the end, only God's knowledge, in which none of us fully share, is true. Perhaps your children's hearts were stopped. Perhaps that is no obstacle for God."

"Thank you," said Simeon.

"I must return," said the midwife. "We need more water. Fill this basin."

The door again closed to him, Simeon looked to the clouds and felt the wind and water on his face. He held the basin before him, collecting the rain as it fell.

"My brother is dead," he said.

'My children are born," he said.

And then he prayed:

Oh divine mystery!
I know not why my children came, nor where my brother went,
but only that the hand of God was there in each event.

Oh hand of God!
I know not why the rain now falls, nor why the land was dry,
but only that the acts of man do oft your will defy.

Oh acts of Man!
I know not how Your will doth play, nor if we there conspire,
but only that we shape Your deeds herein this earthly mire.

Oh deeds of God!
I know not how You formed the world, nor what sustains it still,
but with an ever thankful heart before Your throne I kneel.

The End.

www.ingramcontent.com/pod-product-compliance
Lightning Source LLC
Chambersburg PA
CBHW020329130626
46549CB00003B/1087